HOCUS POCUS DIPLODOCUS

by **Steve Howson**

illustrated by **Kate Daubney**

One hundred and fifty million years ago,

Hocus P. Diplodocus was born.

Even when he was a baby,

Hocus was different...

He sneezed, and his eggshell disappeared

with a loud POP.

"How strange," thought his mummy.

But diplodocuses have very small brains. So she ate some leaves and forgot all about it.

Hocus could do lots of unusual things.

When he flicked his tail, he could make rocks,

trees and even other dinosaurs disappear!

When they appeared again, they were a long way off.

His friends found this very annoying.

Hocus could make a flock of flying

dinosaurs appear.

He was sure he could cut another dinosaur

in half and put them back together again.

But nobody would let him try.

Sometimes, Hocus made things disappear by accident.

Once, when he was about to eat his dinner, a fly buzzed right up his nose.

ATISHOOO!

His dinner vanished!

Then one day... GGRROARR!

A hungry T. Rex rushed out of the forest.

It was just about to gobble up Burpy,

when Hocus flicked his tail...

...and made all of its teeth fall out.

The T. Rex dropped Burpy into a pool
of dribble and ran away.

Burpy let out a big cheer – and a small burp.

"That was amazing!" he cried.

"You should put on a show," said Ian.

"But you need a more interesting name."

"Great idea!" said Hocus. "We could use that 'P' in the middle of my name."

"Yes, we could call you Polly!" said Terry, with a grin.

"Pimplebottom," giggled Burpy.

"I know," cried Stevie, "POCUS!"

Soon it was time for Hocus Pocus Diplodocus to perform the world's first magic show.

Nobody had ever seen anything like it.

After that, Hocus put on special shows every week.

He tried out lots of cool tricks.

His powers grew stronger and stronger.

On his birthday, Hocus Pocus Diplodocus

put on the biggest magic show ever.

Thousands of dinosaurs came to watch.

Hocus gathered his powers.

He felt a tingling from the top of his

nose to the tip of his tail.

But then the tingling in his nose turned into a tickle. Hocus tried to stop it, but it just got worse, until...ATISHOOO!

There was a huge flash of light, and
all the dinosaurs disappeared...

Nobody really knows where they went.

Do you?

Quiz

1. What does the 'P' in Hocus's name stand for?
a) Pocus ✓
b) Polly
c) Paul

2. What happens when Hocus sneezes?
a) Things appear
b) Smoke comes out of his nose
c) Things disappear ✓

3. How does Hocus stop the T.Rex from eating Burpy?
a) He makes its teeth fall out ✓
b) He scares it away
c) He tells it off

4. What day does Hocus put on his biggest show?
a) Monday
b) His birthday ✓
c) National Dinosaur Day

5. What happens when a fly goes up Hocus's nose?
a) The fly vanishes
b) Burpy vanishes
c) Hocus's dinner vanishes ✓

Turn over for answers

Early ★ Reader

Yuck! said the Yak

by Alex English Illustrated by Emma Levey

ISBN 978-1-84886-176-3

Maverick Early Readers

Our early readers have been adapted from the original picture books so that children can make the essential transition from listener to reader.

All of these books have been book banded to the industry standard and edited by a leading educational consultant.

Early ★ Reader

The Black and White Club

by Alice Hemming Illustrated by Kimberley Scott

ISBN 978-1-84886-179-4

Early ★ Reader

A Scarf and a Half

by Amanda Brandon
Illustrated by Catalina Echeverri

ISBN 978-1-84886-177-0

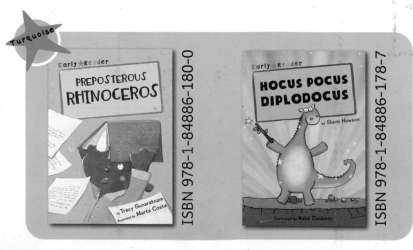

Early ★ Reader

PREPOSTEROUS RHINOCEROS

by Tracy Gunaratnam
Illustrated by Marta Costa

ISBN 978-1-84886-180-0

Early ★ Reader

HOCUS POCUS DIPLODOCUS

by Steve Howson
Illustrated by Kate Daubney

ISBN 978-1-84886-178-7

Quiz Answers:

1a, 2c, 3a, 4b,